This book is dedicated to
My Angel Face,
My Sweet Pea,
My Pumpkin;
My Honey.

And
To all of you kiddos,
Who are going to make
Our world
A better place.
I thank you.

Created by Stephanie Shaffer

Illustrated by Emma Kathryn Akins

One day a boy named Brian and his Dad decided to go to the park to hit some golf balls.

Well, when we take good care of our teeth, brush them well and floss, we make our teeth healthy and strong.

Well remember when you lost your tooth, how you put it under your pillow and the Tooth Fairy left you some money?

Exactly! The Tooth Fairy uses our teeth to help make soil for all the plants, flowers, trees and even the soil for fruits and vegetables! And the whiter, healthier and stronger your teeth are, the prettier and brighter the colors of the flowers, grass and trees will be.

WOW; that is awesome! Dad, what else can I do to make my teeth white and strong besides brushing and flossing?

Well Partner, you can make good choices about what you eat and drink. Brian's Dad continued to explain; when you eat fruits and vegetables, nuts and seeds, and drink water, all those nutrients make your teeth healthy and strong. Then the Tooth Fairy can use them for her soil.

But when you choose to eat candy, junk food and drink soda, your teeth get weak, turn yellow and actually break down. Then the Tooth Fairy is not able to use your teeth for her soil.

"If someone has weak and yellow teeth and the Tooth Fairy can't use them for her soil, what does she do with them?" asked Brian.

Brian's Dad had a puzzled expression come across his face. "You know what Buddy? I really don't know what she does with rotten teeth."

Here's the thing. It's better to focus on what YOU CAN DO to help nature and bring bright colors to the world. When I was a little kid, I always made sure I gave the Tooth Fairy my best effort to give her healthy teeth so she could make strong soil.

Wow Dad, now that I know it is up to me to keep nature bright and full of colors, I am going to make good choices about what I eat and drink. And I am going to brush and floss my teeth EVERY DAY because I want the Tooth Fairy to use MY teeth for her soil!

I think that is a fantastic decision Buddy.